Disney's THE
LION KING
WAY TO GO, SIMBA!

By Ann Braybrooks
Illustrated by Serrat

Golden Books ™ **A GOLDEN BOOK • NEW YORK**

Golden Books Publishing Company, Inc., Racine, Wisconsin 53404

It was a hot day in the jungle. Simba was
playing with Timon the meerkat and Pumbaa
the warthog.

"C'mon," Timon said to the lion cub. "Let's go for a swim."

Simba leaped into the water after his friends.

Splash, splash, splash! They all had fun playing in the cool pond.

Later Timon and Pumbaa settled down for a nap.

But Simba was not sleepy. He saw a
beautiful butterfly and chased after it.

Simba followed the butterfly past a pretty
sunbird sipping from a flower . . .

a family of monkeys chattering in a tree . . .

a bush baby climbing along a branch . . .

and a long green snake slithering across
some rocks.

The butterfly flew from bush to bush.
Simba tried to catch it.

Then the little cub looked around.
"Uh-oh, I'm lost," said Simba. "I shouldn't
have gone off without my friends. But maybe
I can find that snake."

Simba turned and walked back the way he had come. Sure enough, he found the long green snake slithering across some rocks . . .

the bush baby climbing along a branch . . .

the family of monkeys chattering in a tree . . .

and the pretty sunbird sipping from a flower.

And just ahead was the pond! Timon and Pumbaa were waiting for the lion cub.

"Way to go, Simba!" Timon said. "You found us!"

Simba felt proud. "I did it all by myself,"
he said.

Then Simba grinned. "But next time I'm taking you guys with me. The jungle is a lot more fun with friends!"